To all the wonderful trash collectors
who wave at little children like Chase.
—A.Z. & D.C.

To litterbugs everywhere.
—D.Y.

Trashy Town
Text copyright © 1999 by Andrea Zimmerman and David J. Clemesha
Illustrations copyright © 1999 by Dan Yaccarino
Manufactured in China. All rights reserved.
Visit our web site at http://www.harperchildrens.com.

Library of Congress Cataloging-in-Publication Data
Zimmerman, Andrea Griffing.
Trashy Town / by Andrea Zimmerman & David Clemesha; pictures by Dan Yaccarino.
p. cm.   Summary: Little by little, can by can, Mr. Gilly, the trash man, cleans up his town.
ISBN 0-06-027139-6. — ISBN 0-06-027140-X (lib. bdg.)   [1. Refuse and refuse
disposal—Fiction.] I. Clemesha, David. II. Yaccarino, Dan, ill. III. Title.
PZ7.Z618Tr 1999   98-27495
[E]—dc21   CIP
                                                                AC

13 15 17 19 20 18 16 14
❖

TRASHY TOWN

Andrea Zimmerman and David Clemesha
illustrated by Dan Yaccarino

HarperCollins*Publishers*

Mr. Gilly is a trashman.

In the morning, Mr. Gilly puts on his heavy gloves. He climbs into his big trash truck.

He turns the key. He drives his
empty truck down the street.
He is looking for trash.

STOP!

There are trash cans by the school.

Mr. Gilly empties the cans into the truck.

Dump it in, smash it down, drive around the Trashy Town!

Is the trash truck full yet?

NO.

Mr. Gilly drives on.

STOP!

There are trash cans in the <u>park.</u>

Mr. Gilly empties the cans into the truck.

Dump it in, smash it down, drive around the Trashy Town!

Is the trash truck full yet?

NO.

Mr. Gilly drives on.

STOP!

There are trash cans behind the pizza parlor.

Mr. Gilly empties the cans into the truck.

Dump it in, smash it down, drive around the Trashy Town!

Is the trash truck full yet?

NO.

Mr. Gilly drives on.

STOP!

There are trash cans next to the doctor's office.

Mr. Gilly empties the cans into the truck.

Dump it in, smash it down, drive around the Trashy Town!

Is the trash truck full yet?

NO.

Mr. Gilly drives on.

STOP!

There are trash cans by the <u>fire station</u>.

Mr. Gilly empties the cans into the truck.

Dump it in, smash it down, drive around the Trashy Town!

Is the trash truck full yet?

NO.

Mr. Gilly
drives
down
all the
streets
in
Trashy
Town.

He
empties
all the
trash cans
into the
truck.

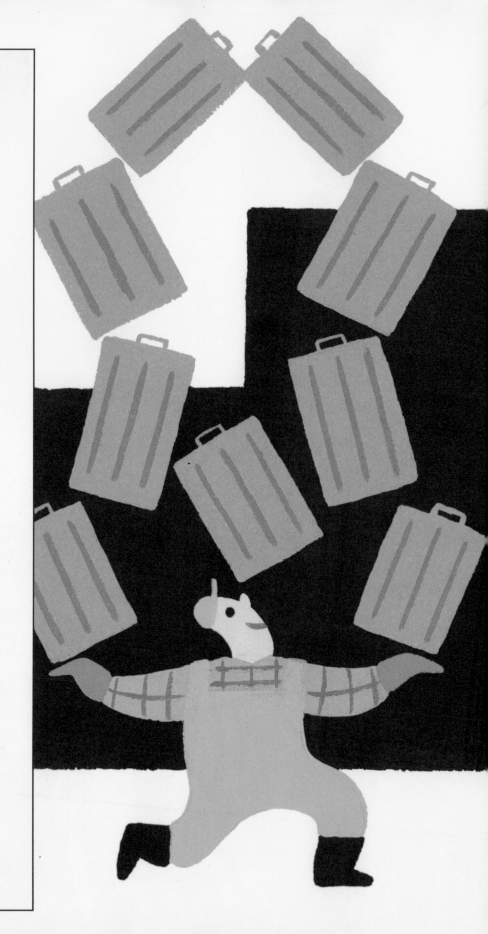

Dump it
in, smash
it down,
drive
around
the Trashy
Town!

Is the
trash
truck full
yet?

YES!

Mr. Gilly has cleaned up
the whole town!

Mr. Gilly drives the full trash truck to the dump.

Up, up, up goes the truck. Down, down, down goes the trash.

I dumped
it in.
I smashed
it down.

I love
to
clean
up
Trashy
Town!

Mr. Gilly turns off the key.
He takes off his gloves.
Then he goes home.

Now there's only one more thing
to clean up . . .

Time for a bath, Mr. Gilly!